Girls Love to Fart

I'd like to say a big thank you to my Mum and Dad for teaching me that farting is okay

Written by Alice Clover
Illustrated by Cheryl Lucas

Copyright © 2019 Alice Clover Stories
Copyright © 2019 Cheryl Lucas Illustration

Some girls fart ever so quietly

And some girls fart very loud

Some girls fart on their own

And some girls fart in a crowd

Some girls fart whilst they're talking

And may even fart when they sing

Sometimes they fart whilst out running

They even fart on the swing

Some girls fart wearing trousers

Or sometimes whilst wearing a dress

They fart whilst playing scrabble

They fart whilst playing chess

Sometimes they fart in the kitchen
Their farts may smell like an egg

They often fart in the playground
Whilst standing on one leg

Girls like to fart whilst dancing

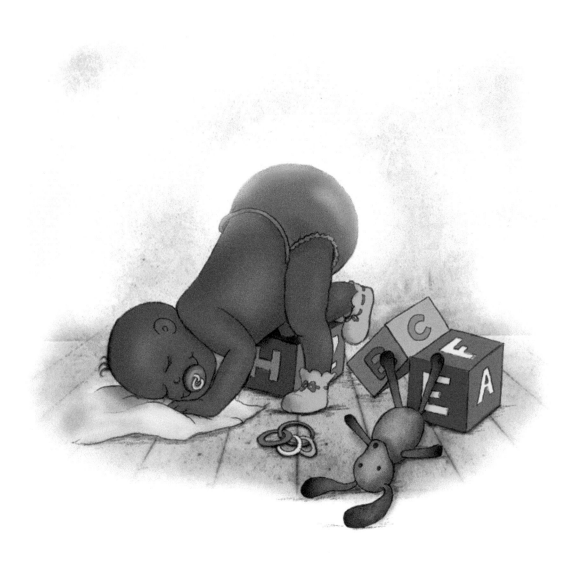

And standing on their head

They fart whilst doing the limbo

And bouncing on the bed

Some girls fart eating pasta
And whilst they're eating toast

They fart out in the garden
They fart if they see a ghost

Girls like to fart at bedtime

It's most fun to fart at night

When everyone else is sleeping

Girls can give them a farty fright

Some girls fart whilst they're walking
And some girls fart in the rain

Some girls fart in the sunshine
and some even fart on a train

Everyone farts at some time
There's no shame in letting one go
Girls can be just as stinky
Be proud and let the world know!

Lightning Source UK Ltd.
Milton Keynes UK
UKHW051007241220
375828UK00003B/53